Ruby's Sleepover

For Suzy, love Mum — K. W.
To Miranda, lots and lots of love xx — M. L.

Barefoot Books
294 Banbury Road
Oxford, OX2 7ED

First published in Great Britain by Barefoot Books, Ltd in 2012
The paperback edition first published in 2012

Graphic design by Judy Linard, London
Reproduction by B & P International, Hong Kong
Printed in China on 100% acid-free paper
This book was typeset in Triplex and Hoagie Infant
The illustrations were prepared in acrylic paints
and watercolour pencils

Hardback ISBN 978-1-84686-592-3
Paperback ISBN 978-1-84686-759-0

British Cataloguing-in-Publication Data:
a catalogue record for this book is available from the British Library

1 3 5 7 9 8 6 4 2

Ruby's Sleepover

Written by **Kathryn White**

Illustrated by **Miriam Latimer**

Barefoot Books
step inside a story

I'm sleeping with Mai in my tent tonight,
When the **moon** is full and the **stars** are bright.

We're both so excited!
We **whoop** and we **jump**,
Into the tent we **tumble** and **bump**.

One bag on this side, one bag on that,
Mai's brought her teddy
and I've brought my cat.

I open my rucksack and show Mai my things:
My **egg**
and my **beans**
and my **magical rings**.

We nibble our snacks
and hear foxes bark.
Then turn on our torches
to see in the **dark**.

The **mOOn** shines above us;

there's no one about.

We snuggle down deep

with our eyes peeking out.

I'm not at all nervous; I feel quite prepared.

'Don't worry,' I say,

'there's no need to be scared.'

But a **rumble** —

a **grumble!** —

roars loud down the street.

Mai grabs my arm and jumps to her feet.

I giggle and say, 'A **giant** is near.'

Mai screeches out,

'Don't let it in here!'

'I'll toss out these **beans**

so they'll grow up so high

That the **giant** can climb

to his home in the sky.'

I hold out the beans and I give them a **shake**.

As the giant gets nearer I feel the earth **quake**.

So I open the tent flap
and throw the beans out.
'Go back to your castle,
this minute!' I shout.

An owl **hoots** a warning from high in the trees.
The tent starts to **rustle** and **shake** in the breeze.

'Did you see that shadow?'

Mai trembles in fright.

I whisper, 'A **dragon** is

coming tonight.'

'And when it comes **huffing**

and **puffing** about,

Snorting out

flames from its

long purple snout,

I'll send it away on a **magical quest**:

It must carry this **egg** safely back to its nest.'

So I open the tent flap and call to the sky,

'Here is your **dragon's egg**, take it and fly.'

I take out my **rings** to keep danger at bay;

I slip one on my finger and give one to Mai.

We can't hear a sound now, not even a peep.

But we feel really brave as the world falls asleep.

Then Mai starts a story
her grandfather told,
Of swashbuckling **pirates**
all hunting for **gold**

With **magical ships** that sail from the **moon**.

I look up and say, 'They'll be flying here soon.'

'And they'll carry us off to scrub the decks clean.

They'll be **rotten** and **smelly**

and **nasty** and **mean**.

They're close to the tent now;

they're creeping around.'

'**Shhh!**' I tell Mai,

'We must **not** make a sound.'

But Mai is asleep,

with a sweet little **snore**.

And I really don't feel quite

as brave as before.

Then **whoosh** goes the tent flap —

My heart gives a leap.

'Wake up, Mai, I need you!'

But Mai's fast asleep.

So I hold out my **ring**

and I scrunch up my eyes,

'Oh wind, take those **pirates**

back up to the skies.

This **magical ring** will not let you near.'

And I point really hard and I say,

'Disappear!'

The tent flap stops moving —

I hug my ring tight.

So **giants**

and **dragons**

and **pirates**,

'Goodnight!'